I'm . . .

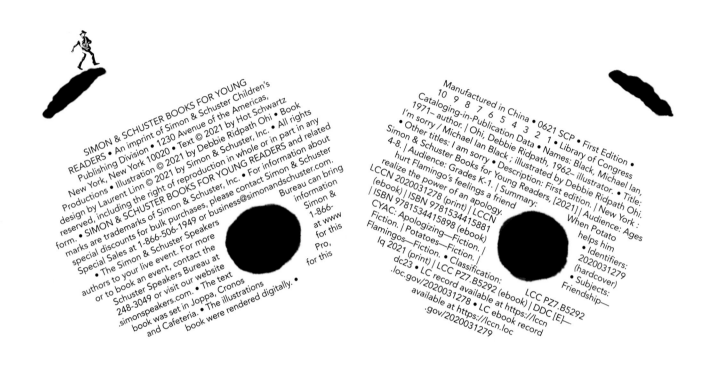

SIMON & SCHUSTER BOOKS FOR YOUNG READERS • An imprint of Simon & Schuster Children's Publishing Division • 1230 Avenue of the Americas, New York, New York 10020 • Text © 2021 by Hot Schwartz Productions • Illustration © 2021 by Debbie Ridpath Ohi • Book design by Laurent Linn © 2021 by Simon & Schuster, Inc. • All rights reserved, including the right of reproduction in whole or in part in any form. • SIMON & SCHUSTER BOOKS FOR YOUNG READERS and related marks are trademarks of Simon & Schuster, Inc. • For information about special discounts for bulk purchases, please contact Simon & Schuster Special Sales at 1-866-506-1949 or business@simonandschuster.com. • The Simon & Schuster Speakers Bureau can bring authors to your live event. For more information or to book an event, contact the Simon & Schuster Speakers Bureau at 1-866-248-3049 or visit our website at www .simonspeakers.com. • The text for this book was set in Joppa, Cronos Pro, and Cafeteria. • The illustrations for this book were rendered digitally. •

Manufactured in China • 0621 SCP • First Edition 10 9 8 7 6 5 4 3 2 1 • Library of Congress Cataloging-in-Publication Data • Names: Black, Michael Ian, 1971– author. | Ohi, Debbie Ridpath. Title: I'm sorry / Michael Ian Black ; illustrated by Debbie Ridpath Ohi. • Other titles: I am sorry • Description: First edition. | New York : Simon & Schuster Books for Young Readers, [2021] | Audience: Ages 4-8. | Audience: Grades K-1. | Summary: When Potato hurt Flamingo's feelings a friend helps him realize the power of an apology. • Identifiers: LCCN 2020031278 (print) | LCCN 2020031279 (ebook) | ISBN 9781534415881 (hardcover) | ISBN 9781534415898 (ebook) | Subjects: CYAC: Apologizing—Fiction. | Friendship— Fiction. | Potatoes—Fiction. | Flamingos—Fiction. • Classification: lq 2021 (print) | LCC PZ7.B5292 dc23 • LC record available at https://lccn .loc.gov/2020031278 • LC ebook record available at https://lccn.loc .gov/2020031279

There's so many people I never said I'm sorry to over the years.
To all of them, I'm sorry. —M. I. B.

For Luisa, dear friend and fellow (apologetic) Canadian.
—D. R. O.

I'M SORRY

By **Michael Ian Black**

Illustrated by **Debbie Ridpath Ohi**

SIMON & SCHUSTER BOOKS FOR YOUNG READERS
New York London Toronto Sydney New Delhi

Flamingo,
are you okay?

Potato hurt my feelings.

Oh no!
But you and Potato
are such good friends.

What happened?

We were having fun
playing superheroes,
but then he said something
really mean.

Oh, Flamingo.

I'll go talk to him.

But that's **SO HARD.**

Saying I'm sorry is maybe
the hardest
thing to say in
the entire world.

Even harder than saying
Solanum tuberosum.

That's a fancy way
of saying potato.

Potato, do you feel sorry?

The sorriest.

And you know
what you did
was wrong?

The wrongiest.

Then you already did the hard part.

Now you just have to tell Flamingo.

I know it's
YOU,
Potato.

Oh.

That I was
only joking
and it
wasn't my fault
and—

Potato.

And . . .

and . . .

and . . .

and . . .

and . . .

You **really**
hurt my feelings.

I know.
I'm sorry.

And I **still**
feel pretty upset.

I'm so sorry.

I feel really, really bad about it and
I know there's nothing I can do to
take it back, but I hope, one day,
we can be friends again.

Guess I'll just take my really cool cowboy costume and go. . . .

Potato?
It might be nice if we had somebody else to play with.

ME!

ME!

ME!

And it might be nice if I had
a hug from my friend.

Me?